# A Pony Named Midnight

by Susan Taylor Brown

illustrations by Linda Sniffen

For Danielle
& Jarrod,
Happy reading!
It was so nice
to meet you.
Susan Taylor Brown

published by **WRITERS PRESS**

For my daughter Jennifer,
in memory of
Sheikh, Mystique, Jasmine
and the blind pony Sonny,
who helped her first learn to ride.

*Susan Taylor Brown*

4

Today was Heather's first day of horse camp. They would practice all week. Then they would have a horse show.

Heather sat on the fence and watched the horses. A small, brown horse ate some hay. A big, yellow horse swished his tail at the flies. A black pony ran under a tree. He looked like he was playing tag.

"Do you want to ride a horse or a pony?" asked Debbie, the camp leader.

"I want to ride the black pony," said Heather. "He is just my size. We will be a good team."

Debbie nodded. "Teamwork is important when you ride a horse. Especially when you ride Midnight."

"Why?" asked Heather.

"Midnight is blind. You will have to be his eyes."

Heather shook her head no. "I don't want to ride a pony who can't see."

"He was born blind," said Debbie, "just like some people. But you can still ride Midnight, just like you ride the other horses"

"No," said Heather. "I will ride the big, yellow horse."

The yellow horse was named Taffy.

Heather went to the tack room. Thats where they keep the saddles and blankets and brushes.

Heather got a soft brush. She brushed Taffy's sides. She brushed Taffy's legs.

Heather put the blanket on Taffy's back. She could not lift the saddle up high enough. Debbie put the saddle on Taffy. Debbie showed Heather how to fasten the cinch so the saddle would not fall off. Then Debbie put the bit in Taffy's mouth.

"Now you are ready to ride," said Debbie. She helped Heather up into the saddle.

Heather looked down. The ground was far away. She thought about Midnight. He was just her size. She could have reached Midnight's back. She could have put the saddle on by herself. She could have gotten on without help.

But Midnight was blind. Heather didn't know anyone who was blind.

Taffy would not move.

"Kick harder," said Debbie. "You won't hurt her. Sometimes Taffy is lazy."

Heather kicked harder. Taffy still would not move.

Debbie slapped Taffy on the side. "Come on, Taffy," she said. "It's time to go on the trail."

Taffy started to walk. She walked very slow. Heather could not catch up with her friends.

The horses climbed over a hill. They came to a creek. All the other horses walked through the creek, but not Taffy.

"Come on, Taffy," said Heather. "Water can't hurt you."

Taffy stopped and took a drink from the creek. She would not walk through it. Debbie had to help again. Heather was glad when they went back to the barn.

Barrel racing was next. Everyone took turns going as fast as they could around the barrels.

Heather waited for Debbie to say go. Then she gave Taffy a kick and made a clicking sound with her tongue.

"Run, Taffy, run," she said.

But Taffy would not run. She just trotted. When they got to the first barrel, Taffy stopped. Heather used the reins to tell Taffy to turn. Taffy went backwards instead.

Heather let Taffy walk backwards to the fence.

"I want to ride a different horse now," she told Debbie. "Taffy doesn't like to do anything."

"I'm sorry Heather," said Debbie. "There is no other horse to ride."

"What about Midnight?" asked Heather.

"Sure, but Midnight is still blind."

"I'm scared," whispered Heather. "I don't know what to do."

"It's okay to be scared about something you don't understand, you'll learn," said Debbie. "Midnight will not hurt you. If you work together, you will be surprised what Midnight can do. Let's work on it!"

Heather tied Midnight up by the barn. Then she went to the tack room for a brush.

She brushed Midnight's sides. She brushed Midnight's legs. She even brushed his back.

"I was right," Heather told Midnight. "You are just my size."

Then it was time to saddle up. Heather put the blanket on Midnight's back. Next she put the saddle on top of the blanket. Debbie helped fasten the cinch.

Heather put the reins on Midnight and even put the bit in his mouth.

Now they were ready.

"We make a good team," Heather told Midnight.

Heather rode Midnight all day. Out on the trail with the other campers, Heather guided Midnight right through the creek. He did not even slow down. They practiced racing the barrels and they learned teamwork.

The next day was the horse show. Midnight was excited. He pawed the ground. He swished his tail. He wanted to do the speed barrels.

Heather waited for Debbie to say go. Then she gave Midnight a little kick.

The pony ran to the first barrel. When Heather pulled on the reins to turn him, Midnight turned. He ran to the next barrel and turned again.

It didn't matter that Midnight could not see. He trusted Heather to be his eyes. They were a good team.

They turned past the last barrel.

"Faster, Midnight," said Heather. "Faster, faster!"

Midnight and Heather raced past the finish line. They beat Katy and Max. Heather won the blue ribbon!

"The blue ribbon really belongs to you," Heather told Midnight. She hung the ribbon around his ear. Then she gave him a big hug.

"But maybe," she whispered, "you would like to trade me the blue ribbon for this nice juicy apple."